Melodie Campbell

PIZZA WARS

Melodie Campbell, called the "Queen of Comedy" by *The Toronto Sun,* got her start writing standup. She now has more than 200 publications: 100 comedy credits, 60 short stories, and 20 novels including the award-winning book *The Goddaughter's Revenge.* Her bestselling *Rowena Through the Wall* series was an Amazon Top 50 bestseller. *Pizza Wars* is Melodie's twenty-first book. And yes, she comes from an Italian family.

First published by Gemma in 2026.

www.gemmamedia.org

Printed in the United States of America

978-1-956476-54-5

Library of Congress Cataloging-in-Publication Data

Names: Campbell, Melodie author
Title: Pizza wars / Melodie Campbell.
Identifiers: LCCN 2026005843 (print) | LCCN 2026005844
(ebook) | ISBN 9781956476545 paperback |
ISBN 9781956476552 epub
Subjects: LCGFT: Detective and mystery fiction | Novels
Classification: LCC PR9199.4.C3497 P59 2026 (print) |
LCC PR9199.4.C3497 (ebook)
LC record available at https://lccn.loc.gov/2026005843
LC ebook record available at https://lccn.loc.gov/2026005844

Cover by Laura Shaw Design

Gemma's Open Doors provide fresh stories, new ideas, and essential resources for young people and adults as they embrace the power of reading and the written word.

DAY 1

Chapter One

Ben took a big breath. Today was the first day of a new job in Steeltown. It was exciting, but also scary.

He looked up at the big red brick building in front of him. This is where he had dreamed of working since he had been a kid. This is what he had trained for.

He walked up the wide concrete steps. Ben summoned all his courage. He pushed open the door to the police station.

He first heard the racket. People yacking, phones ringing, keyboards clacking. It was one thing you could count on in every police station: constant noise.

"Hi! Are you the new guy?" a voice hollered across the room.

He nodded, and walked over to the desk.

A pretty blond woman looked up. She had a great smile. "I'm Patty. Welcome to Elm Street Police Station." She looked over her shoulder. "Hey Sarge, the new guy is here."

A bunch of heads looked up from desks and poked around corners.

"Hi, new guy," said someone. A few snickered.

Ben didn't like being the new guy. You're the outsider. Everybody knows everyone else, except you. He'd been the new guy in high school. And again at police college. He knew that feeling well.

An older man came out from behind a wall. His blue uniform fit him snugly. He had gray hair and wore the right stripes.

"So you're the new guy. Ben Black, is it?" He smiled and held out a hand. "Welcome to Elm Street. I'm Sargeant Ryan. You can call me Sarge."

Ben took the hand and shook it. He stood as tall as he could, which was pretty tall. Taller even than the man in front of him. "Yes, sir. Thank you, sir!"

"You play basketball?" said Sarge.

Ben sighed and nodded. Everyone asked that.

"Good. We got a team. Mom, get over here!" said Sarge.

Mom?

"She'll be your partner, to start," said Sarge.

"Your mom?" Ben couldn't believe it. Wasn't this against the rules?

Sarge chuckled. "No, no. We just call her that. You'll find out why."

A woman stepped out from behind the half wall. Brown hair and brown eyes. Stocky, mid-height, and tough. The buttons on her uniform looked ready to burst. Ben figured they didn't dare.

"Is he old enough to drive?" she said.

Sarge chuckled. "You wouldn't let him drive anyway."

She shrugged. Then she turned to Ben. "What do they call you, besides new guy?"

"Ben Black," he said.

"You're awful thin. Don't they feed you?" she said.

"Now, now, Mom. Don't go making the poor guy nervous on his first day." Sarge turned to Ben. "This here is Officer Gallo. She'll show you the ropes."

Officer Gallo frowned. "Right now?"

"Sure," said Sarge. "Why? Are you headed out?"

Officer Gallo nodded. "Someone called in another pizza delivery robbery. You want I should take him along?"

Sarge looked thoughtful. "Yeah," he said. "Pizza pilfering. How dangerous could that be?"

Ben was soon to find out.

Chapter Two

"My first name is Rita," said Officer Gallo. "You can call me that. Or Mom. This is my squad car. I'll drive."

She led Ben over to a beat-up police car. It made Ben wonder if maybe he should drive.

It was a nice fall day. The steel plants were bellowing out gray smoke into a blue sky. The leaves were starting to turn yellow and red. You could wear your uniform and not roast to death. Ben was cheerful.

He got into the passenger seat and put on his seat belt. This was the moment he had been waiting for. His first call out with his first partner.

"Thanks, Rita." Ben couldn't call her Mom, at least not right away. It seemed too personal.

"For what?" Rita said. She shifted the car into gear with a clunk and backed up fast.

Ben had to think about it. "For taking me on."

"Oh, that," said Rita. The car peeled out of the parking lot. "I get all the newbies. Like they need a woman's soft touch, you know?"

A woman's soft touch? Ben had to stifle a snort. Rita seemed about as soft as a bulldog. So why did they call her Mom?

"This pizza heist. You hear about that?" Rita smashed the horn with her fist. "Who taught you to drive?" She yelled out the window. "Your grand-mother?"

Ben braced himself for the sudden stop that didn't come.

Rita continued. "So here's the thing. Someone's knocking over pizza delivery boys. Whomping them good, and stealing the pizzas."

"Pizzas? More than one?" *So not just someone who is hungry*, Ben thought.

Rita glanced over. "You gotta realize this is Steeltown. Pizza is an important commodity in this town. Almost a symbol, you know? Ti-Cats, pizza, and beer. You don't mess with any of them."

Ben knew the Ti-Cats were a football team. He also knew there were a lot of Italians in Steeltown. And beer—well, this was Canada, after all. You didn't mess with Canada. Or Canadian beer.

*

Ben was quiet. He thought about this town as he looked out the window. All those tall buildings going by! Ben wasn't from Steeltown. He didn't know the streets well. They didn't have many where he came from. You didn't need many roads where there were more cows than cars.

To him, this was "the City." He'd been excited to be assigned here. And he really didn't want to mess up.

The car thumped to a stop. Ben's hands hit the dashboard. *Good thing for seat belts,* he thought. He got out of the car.

Rita had parked in front of a run-down old house. The snot green paint was peeling. The stairs up to the porch leaned in different directions. The weeds needed cutting.

Rita went up to the door and knocked fiercely. Nothing. She knocked again.

"Yeah, yeah, I'm coming," said a young voice.

The door opened. A kid of about nine years old stood in the doorway.

"Oh, it's you," he said to Rita. "Dad's not here. He's in—"

"Jail, I know." Rita said. "I'm Officer Gallo, and this here is Officer Black."

The kid grinned. "Yer not black, yer brown!"

"Hey, mind your manners!"

"Ah, take a pill," the kid said.

"You kiss your mother with that mouth?" She pulled something from her weapons belt and waved it through the air.

A wooden spoon?

"OK, OK!" said the kid, backing up. "No need for the spoon. You want Paulo, right? About the pizzas?" He looked over his shoulder. "Hey, Paulo! Officer Mom wants to talk to you."

He gave Rita a lopsided smile and then took off down the road.

Rita holstered the spoon. *So that's why they call her Mom,* Ben thought. He shivered.

The young man called Paulo limped into the hall. "They got me again, Mom. They took two large meat-lovers and a Hawaiian."

"How many times is this?" asked Rita. "You first. Then…?"

"Then Marco, yesterday," he said. "Then me again. Sucks."

"How many of them?" asked Mom.

"At least two. Maybe three, wearing ninja turtle masks. They knocked over my bike and then kicked me. Destroyed the bike."

"That's awful!" said Ben. "What type of bike was it?" He loved motor-cycles.

"I don't know." Paulo shrugged. "CCM? Canadian Tire? The kind with two wheels. I didn't buy it myself."

"That's because it was stolen," said Rita.

Uh oh! The wooden spoon came out again.

Paulo back away. "Wasn't me! I didn't do nothing!"

"Anything." She corrected, still holding the spoon. "Honestly. I gotta speak to your mother about your grammar."

"She ain't here. She's in—"

"Jail. I know," said Rita.

Chapter Three

Back in the squad car, Rita explained.

"Paulo works for his uncle Tony. He owns Tony O's, one of the best pizza places in town. And this is a town with a lot of good pizza. We'll go there next."

As Rita clunked the car into gear, Ben wondered. Should he ask? Or should he wait for her to speak? It was hard to know what to do.

"So you might be wondering why someone is hijacking pizzas," she said.

Bingo! Now he had an opening.

"Exactly," he said. "Are they homeless? Hungry? Or is it something bigger?"

"Good start." Rita nodded. "Last time, we found some boxes dropped off outside the homeless shelter on Main. We'll go there later. But first I want to talk to Tony. I'm pretty sure this is bigger than bacon and double cheese."

Rita turned a corner and then pulled up in front of a restaurant. The name above the door said Tony O's, in red neon letters.

"What's the O stand for?" Ben asked.

"Orso," said Rita. "It means 'bear.' That's why he just went with just O. Not a great image for a family place."

Ben wasn't sure about that. *What about the A&W Root Bear? It was friendly. The Pizza Bear? OK, maybe not.*

Rita turned off the car. "Tony's mother was my aunt's cousin's hairdresser. So we're pretty close."

Ben nodded. *Hairdressers are important in a big place like Steeltown. Sort of like donuts. Now, a hairdressing salon with donuts. Why had nobody thought of that?*

Rita beckoned him out of the car. She led the way into the pizza shop. Ben looked around. Lots of paintings on the walls. The leaning tower of Pisa and Roman ruins, that sort of thing.

Sure smells good in here.

At this time of the day, it was nearly empty. Two middle-aged people were cleaning tables, a man and a woman.

"Hey, Leo! Hey, Donna! How are things?" said Rita.

They all rushed forward. Kiss, kiss, kiss.

Ben stood back, figuring Rita would introduce him after the kiss-fest.

And so she did. "This here is Ben Black. He's a good guy, so be nice to him."

"Black," said Leo, musing. "That seems a bit weird, considering."

"I'm brown." Ben sighed. He was used to it.

"And he plays basketball!"

"Well, then." Leo extended a hand and pumped Ben's with vigor. "Any friend of Mom's is a friend of ours." He pulled Ben in for a bear hug with a short "bear." Leo was hardly taller than Rita.

Now Ben was really confused. *Is Rita actually this guy's mom? Or did everyone call her that?*

"So what's this I hear about hijacked pizzas?" Rita asked.

"Oh, Rita. It's awful. You gotta talk to Tony. Hey, Tony!" Donna yelled in a voice barely above a canon blast.

A heavyset man came out from behind the counter. He was wiping his hands on a white tea towel.

"Rita, Rita, they are going to ruin me!" More kisses, both cheeks.

"Who, Tony? Who?" Rita asked. She pushed back, looking serious.

"Those slimy Meatsa Pizza people. Always trying to ruin my business! You go talk to Vinnie. He's had it in for me ever since senior prom. I can't help it that I married his girlfriend."

What? thought Ben. *This whole thing is about senior prom in…what? 1985?*

"There, there," said Rita, patting Tony on the shoulder. "Vera wouldn't let him do this."

"Crummy pizza," he grumbled. "They don't even use fresh oregano! No wonder Vera picked me."

Rita nodded. "Meatsa ain't the besta."

"You go there, Rita! You tell Vinnie to lay off my delivery guys." He pointed a finger. "Or this is going to get nasty."

Nasty? Like in a war? Ben thought. *Pizza Wars. How do you fight a pizza war? Pepperoni sticks at thirty paces?*

"We're on it," said Rita. "You tell Vera not to worry."

Tony shook his head. "You hungry? I got calzone. You wait." He disappeared into the back.

Rita turned to Ben. "He makes the best calzone. It's easier to eat in the car than pizza."

Ben cheered up. The smell in the place was driving him nuts.

Tony returned with two bags. He handed one to each of them. They smelled heavenly.

"Forty years!" Tony cried. He waved his arms around. "You think he'd give up after forty years."

"Vera's never going to leave you." Rita patted Tony on the shoulder again. "She knows a good sauce when she sees one."

Chapter Four

Back in the squad car, Ben spoke up. "This had been going on for 40 years? Seriously?"

Rita clunked the car into gear. "You gotta know Italians, Ben. The Roman empire was kicking butt over 2,000 years ago. Seems like yesterday to the Romans. Forty years is a mere week ago."

Ben was impressed. Most days, he couldn't remember what he had for dinner the night before.

Rita pulled onto King Street. "'Course, it never got this serious before. Used to be petty comments in church on Sunday. Missing prayer books and broken rosaries. Once there was a food fight at a funeral. You know. Normal stuff."

This was a new meaning of the word "normal" that Ben hadn't heard before.

"This is the first time they've attacked a business. Crazy! Vera will be furious when she hears." Rita turned a corner. "You don't want to get Vera mad. She's built like a brick wall."

Her voice had a quiver in it.

She paused at a light. "Nah, that's not it. This isn't about the prom. Something more serious is going on here. I can feel it."

*

They ate their calzone back at the station parking lot. (Not inside, as that would have been crazy.)

"Everyone's a mooch. If you don't have enough to share, you gotta lay low," said Rita. "We'll eat in the car. But don't worry. I'll introduce you to everyone in the station later."

Ben was grateful for Rita's advice. She was right about the calzone, too. It might have been the best thing he'd ever eaten. *Ever.*

When they were finished munching, Ben spoke. "We visit this Vinnie guy next?"

"Hey, Rita!" yelled someone outside the car. Rita put the window down all the way.

A stocky young guy in uniform poked his head down so he could see into the car. He had curly dark hair and a friendly smile.

"Is that from Tony O's?" he asked.

"Sorry, Gino," said Rita. "He only gave us one each. I didn't know you were working today."

"That's OK. The wife has me on a diet." He patted his ample belly.

"This here is my new partner, Ben." Rita motioned to him with her free hand.

"Welcome aboard!" said Gino. "Are you two working on the pizza case?"

"Yeah. You know anything about it?" Rita asked.

Gino straightened and shrugged. "I don't think it's Meatsa Pizza. Vinnie didn't do it. He seems as puzzled as anyone."

"Vinnie is Gino's uncle," Rita explained.

Ben rolled his eyes. *Is everybody in this town related to everyone else?*

"And you know Vinnie," said Gino. "He usually likes to boast about the crappy things he does."

Rita looked thoughtful. "There is that. He did start the food fight at Big Sally's funeral, after all."

"And never stops talking about it." Gino agreed. "The dry cleaners did a great business that week. My uncle was happy."

"Gino's uncle owns Capri Cleaners," Rita explained to Ben. "Of course, he has a lot of businesses. And a lot of uncles."

Ben rolled his eyes again.

Rita frowned. "But if not Vinnie, then who?"

"I don't know," said Gino, scratching his chin. "Maybe one of those anti-meat types? The people who protest about pepperoni on pizza? Ban the Beef is one. They sometimes leave leaflets."

"Good idea," said Rita. "We'll follow it up."

Gino looked at Ben. "Nice to meet you," he said. "See you around the station later." Then he saluted and sauntered away, toward the station.

Rita finished her calzone before she tried to talk. Then she said, "Ban the Beef—that's a good lead. We should check them out. I only have one question first."

Ben had been thinking while munching, too. He said, "Why would they pick on Tony O's? If they are against meat, surely they would pick on—"

"Meatsa Pizza first. Exactly. It's right in the name," said Rita. "So I got some questions. Let's go get some answers."

Chapter Five

When they were done eating, Ben gathered up the garbage.

Rita pointed out the bin, at the side of the building. "You got young legs," she said.

Ben didn't mind. It felt good to do something useful. When he got back to the squad car, he asked, "So where do we go next?"

"I'm thinking we should track down those Ban the Beef people next," said Rita. "I'd like to rule them out."

"How do we do that?" Ben asked. "Don't those groups usually want to stay underground?"

"Bah," said Rita, waving a hand. "My cousin's daughter's boyfriend is one of the leaders. I can find out where they hang out."

"Of course he is," muttered Ben. *Was there anybody in this town she wasn't related to?*

Rita pulled out a cell phone. She punched a few numbers and waited. "Hey, Rosina. It's Rita. How's the family? Yeah…yeah… How's Manny's constipation?"

Ben choked on air.

"Good. I told you prunes would work. Hey, I need to find the Ban the Beef people. Anna's boyfriend still part of that? Yeah… yeah… great. Thank you. See you at church on Sunday. I got a new hat." She clicked off.

Rita turned to Ben. "Ban the Beef meets in a small room behind the Humane Society on King Street."

"Makes sense," said Ben.

"They volunteer at the society, see?" Rita shifted the car into gear. "Walking the dogs and playing with the cats. They get lonesome, those cats."

"That also makes sense," said Ben. He admired people who worked with animals. It was a kind thing to do.

"I'm not convinced," said Rita. "Usually, this group is non-violent. While I can see them stealing pizzas—everyone loves pizza—I just can't see them trashing a bike. Or kicking a poor delivery guy when he's down. It's not like he runs the joint."

"I see what you mean," said Ben. "Except he's an easy target. All alone, riding a bike."

"There's that," agreed Rita. She turned onto King. Ben watched the streets, trying to memorize where each one connected with the next. He'd check a map on his phone when he got home. The sooner he learned his way around Steeltown, the better.

"Here it is." Rita turned into the driveway. "Holy cow, this is crowded. It must be one of those Free Cat Days."

The parking lot was full. Cars were circling around, double parked, and blocking the laneway. Rita pulled up right in front, in a no-stopping zone.

"Come on," she said to Ben. "This is the one advantage of being a cop. You can park where no one else can. And the free donuts."

Ben got out of the squad car. He was pretty sure they didn't have free donuts at a Humane Society. Or maybe they did. This was a weird town.

Rita had already raced up to the door. Ben followed her in.

"Hey, Trudy. This is a madhouse," she said. People were everywhere, holding cats and talking to staff members. The room had a peculiar smell. Ben knew that smell. What was it? Something musty combined with strong cleaner. It reminded him of school bathrooms. Not something he really wanted to remember.

The woman at the desk looked up with a smile. She had light brown hair and friendly eyes. "Free Cat Day," she said. "Want a donut?" She pointed to the plate on the desk. "Or a kitten?"

"No donuts. No kittens. Not today. We're here on police business, Trudy," Rita said. "Did you hear about Tony O's delivery boys being attacked?"

"Terrible thing," said Trudy, shaking her head. "What is *wrong* with people these days?"

Ben watched as a tan and white cat crawled across the desk, trailing hair everywhere. *Fur-covered donuts,* he thought with a shiver.

"Are the Ban the Beef people still working out of here?" Rita asked. "I gotta ask them a few questions."

Trudy grabbed the roaming cat. "I think one is today. Behind the kennels," she said. "That way." She nodded with her head.

"Thanks." Rita headed off in that direction.

"Are you sure you don't want a cat?" Trudy yelled after her. "We have eighty-five."

Chapter Six

Ben followed Rita behind the kennels to a little room. There was a sign on the door. It said, "Friendship Room."

Rita explained. "This is where they try to socialize the new cats when they come in. Cats aren't all that friendly to each other at first. You can't let them loose without supervision. The room does double duty for the Ban the Beef people."

Rita didn't bother to knock before she walked in. Ben followed, looking around. This room smelled a bit, but it wasn't too bad. A few small cats were stalking each other, like baby lions. They were really cute. A single young male sat at a desk, looking at his phone. Male human, that is.

"There you are. Rosina told me you volunteered here. I got a question for you. Are you still with Ban the Beef?" Rita asked.

The young guy looked up. When he saw the blue uniform, he sighed. "Oh, it's you, Mom. Yeah, I'm still with Ban the Beef. You got a beef with that?"

Ben covered a chuckle with a cough.

"Funny guy," said Rita. She fingered the wooden spoon on her weapons belt. "You heard about the pizza heists?"

"The delivery guy who got mugged? What about it?" he asked.

Ben sized him up. *Black hair, probably just learned to shave. Maybe*

140 pounds soaking wet. Not a lot of muscle. Only works out on his phone.

"Any chance Ban the Beef is behind it?" Rita asked.

The guy looked shocked. "Are you crazy? We don't do stuff like that. We're not like that other group, Protect the Pork."

Ben nodded. They had a dirty reputation.

"Also, why would we hit Tony O's? They're not the worst. At least they donate to the Humane Society. They help animals." The scrawny guy picked up one of the kittens. "Not like Meatsa Pizza."

He has a point, Ben had to admit.

"Plus they have a killer vegetarian pizza. Why would we target them?"

The fellow stroked the kitten. "Not to mention the obvious point. The operation was too low-key. Why bother?"

Rita gave him a death stare. Then she relaxed. "Nah, I didn't think so. It's OK, Ben. It's not them."

Ben was puzzled. He was glad to hear it. He liked people who helped animals. Still, that was awful fast. "How do you know?" he asked.

Rita smiled. She looked at the guy at the desk. "You want to tell him?" she asked.

The guy cuddling the kitten looked at her, then at him, and then shrugged. "If we did it, you'd know it. We'd be advertising it all over town." He stared up into Ben's eyes. "What's the point of protesting if no one knows why you're doing it? Or who is doing it?"

The light finally dawned on Ben. "I see what you mean. You want the credit when you take the risk."

"Otherwise, why are you doing it?" The young guy grinned. "It's all about getting publicity. Putting your cause in front of people's faces. We do that by social media now. In-person vandalism is for old farts."

Ben wondered when he would be considered an old fart. At thirty-one?

Rita turned to go. "Say 'hello' to your mama for me. And tell Anna I like her new hairstyle." Rita waved an arm and then walked out of the room.

Ben stood staring after her.

"You must be new. Has Mom used that wooden spoon on anyone yet?" asked the scrawny guy.

"Not yet," said Ben. "But it's only been one day."

He followed her out.

Chapter Seven

Back in the squad car, Rita looked at the clock. "It's getting close to three. We probably have time to check out Vinnie's. Then go back to the office and write up the report. We're always writing reports." She gave a deep sigh.

Ben didn't mind. He liked writing reports. At least you felt like you had done something. It made him feel good. You finished a report, even if it was to say you had nothing to report.

As they traveled along Main Street, Rita told him about Meatsa Pizza.

"Used to be Tony and Vinnie worked together at the same pizza joint when they were kids. They were great pals. Then the school prom happened, and Vera came between them. So when Tony O set up his own pizza joint, Vinnie decided to set up in competition. The feud has been going on ever since."

Ben couldn't stop himself from asking. "How exactly do you have a pizza feud?"

Rita turned a corner, nearly clipping a pedestrian. "Wait for the walk signal!" she yelled out the window. Two high school boys jumped. "Rookies," she muttered.

Ben shut his eyes.

Rita continued. "Easy. Meatsa undercuts Tony's price. Tony sends out coupons. Someone posts a bunch of bad reviews on Yelpers. Everyone in town has to pick sides. Or pretend to. I hear there is a lot of underground ordering of pizzas. People use false names." Rita cluck-clucked. "Thing is, we really don't want to let this get out of hand—"

Before she could finish the sentence, a voice came over the car radio. Rita pulled to the curb and picked up the speaker.

"Gallo here," she said. "Yeah… yeah. I'm on it. Where…behind the? On my way."

She hung up.

"Another pizza robbery. Do up your seat belt, Ben. We're gonna fly!"

*

Rita turned onto a narrow side street off Barton. When they got to the crime scene, the car skidded to a stop. A small group of people had gathered.

Rita bolted out of the squad car. Ben followed her.

A discarded bicycle lay flat on the road. A guy was holding his face and sobbing. He looked about eighteen. A middle-aged police officer was helping him sit up.

"Aw, Marco, are you OK?" Rita rushed right over to him.

"Mom! Is that you? I can't see. They hit me with bear spray!" He sneezed. And sneezed again.

"Someone give the guy a tissue," said a bystander.

A matronly woman pulled a wad of tissues out of her black handbag. She held them out.

"He can't see them," Rita said. She grabbed the wad from the woman and shoved them at Marco's chest. "Here, honey. Take these."

A siren split the air.

"Here comes the ambulance," said Louie.

Ben looked to his left. A city ambulance came roaring up, lights flashing. It weaved around the squad car and stopped with a thud. Two people jumped out of the back and raced over.

Marco couldn't stop crying and sneezing. It looked like he had also hurt his leg. It was twisted in a funny direction.

One of the paramedics knelt beside him. "Andy here will find something to sooth your eyes," she said. "I'll give you a shot for the pain." She reached into her medic bag.

Ben could see Rita starting to steam with anger. "You treat him well!" She yelled at the paramedics. "He's a good guy! He didn't deserve this, the poor doofus."

While they fussed over Marco, Rita turned to the officer. "Louie, were you first on the scene?"

The older officer nodded.

"Did you find out what happened?" Rita asked.

Louie nodded again. "Same MO as last time. Two masked guys clipped him when he turned a corner. They kicked out the bike, and took him down. One of them used the spray on his face. Then they stole the pizzas and took off." Louie looked disgusted. "How could they leave the poor guy, in this shape? Who would do this?"

"Did any of you people witness this?" Rita spoke to the crowd of people who had gathered.

Everyone shook their heads.

One elderly man put up his hand. "I heard him scream and came out of my house." He pointed to an old narrow row house. The door had been left wide open. "But they had already driven away."

"In a car?" Rita asked.

The old guy shrugged. "I didn't see."

"If they were taking away pizzas, they were probably in a car," Ben said. "Pizza boxes are pretty hard to hold on a motorcycle."

"Good thinking, Ben," said Rita. She patted him on the shoulder. It made him feel good.

"Marco said they came up from behind," said Louie. "Like they'd been following him. Marco didn't see them until he was down. And then he couldn't, on account of the bear spray in his eyes."

Rita's face was grim. "Still no sign of who they are working for?" she asked.

Louie shook his head.

"They used bear spray so he couldn't identify them," said Rita, in a knowing voice. "Clever, but nasty. That stuff is evil. It blinds you and hurts like hell. They're upping their game."

Ben felt a chill. "Anybody see where the pizzas went?" he asked. Everyone shook their heads.

They all watched as Marco was loaded onto a stretcher.

"Good question, Ben," said Rita. "If we can trace where the pizzas went, maybe somebody saw the thugs. They could give us a better description of them."

"But where do you even start to look?" asked Louie.

Rita turned to Ben. "You got an idea, partner?"

Ben could hardly contain his excitement. "I know! The homeless shelter on Main!"

Rita's mouth stretched to a grin. "Good thinking. You learn fast. Hop in, and let's ride!"

They both raced back to the squad car.

Chapter Eight

"You're awful quiet. Penny for your thoughts," said Rita as they wound their way through town.

Ben smiled at the expression. His grandmother used to say it. Not that you could buy anything for a penny these days…

He did have a question for his partner, though. "Those thugs didn't steal the pizzas just to give them to the homeless, did they?"

"Of course not," said Rita. She sped through a yellow light. "Someone is out to ruin Tony O's business. I just don't believe it is Meatsa Pizza. Or Ban the Beef."

Ben gave it more thought. "Do you suppose we could get fingerprints off the boxes, if we find them?"

"It's possible," Rita said. The car lurched around a corner. "Those boxes might have a lot of different finger-prints on them now, though. After everyone has taken their slices out, the early prints probably got smeared."

Ben had to agree. It seemed like a long shot. Maybe someone had seen the car that dropped the pizzas off?

He had another thought. "They can't be all bad. At least they give the pizzas to people who need it."

"Don't count your chickens before they've hatched, Ben. We don't know that yet." Rita pulled into a narrow alley. "Just because they did it the first time…"

Ben got the message. It wouldn't be smart to follow the same pattern all the time. That's how suspects got caught. He learned that at police school.

Rita stopped the car and opened the door to get out. "The shelter is over there," she said. "It's run by the Sisters of St. Joseph. We can go in the back way."

She led the way, winding through picnic tables outside. A few people sat there, enjoying the sun. No one was munching on pizza.

Rita walked up the rickety wooden steps to the back door. She pulled open the screen door and walked right in.

A gray-haired woman was sweeping the floor. "Is Sister Margaret about?" Rita asked her.

"First door on the right," said the woman. She waved a hand.

Ben followed Rita into a small office. A middle-aged nun wearing a light-colored summer habit was sitting behind an old wooden desk.

"Rita!" cried the nun. "It's been ages!"

"Mags! How the heck are ya?" Rita held out her arms.

They met in a fierce hug. Then the kisses started.

"How are Ernesto and the kids?" Sister Margaret asked.

"Fine, just fine," said Rita. "And your brother's brood? Any more babies?"

"Almost enough for a soccer team now," she responded, with a laugh. "You'll stay for tea, right?"

Wait a minute, thought Ben. *Did Rita have a husband and kids?*

They chatted happily for a few minutes. Ben looked around the room. The desk was a mess of paperwork. He didn't see a computer anywhere, not even a laptop. *I guess this place is old-school,* he thought.

A large cross was on the wall behind the rickety desk. Worn steel file cabinets stood on either side of the one window. A wooden guest chair sat in front of the desk. The rest of the room was lined with boxes pushed against the walls.

He heard Rita pop the question.

Sister Margaret shook her head. "No, we didn't receive any pizzas today. Which is too bad. We can always use fresh food. Most of what we get donated is cans. Not to mention I could really go for some pizza at the moment."

She looked thoughtful. "Are you here about the pizza robberies? I heard about it on the radio. So those pizzas we got were actually stolen? I didn't realize that at the time. They were really good, too." She sounded wistful. "It's hard to imagine people would steal pizzas just to give them to us."

Rita waved a hand at Ben. "This here is my new partner, Ben Black. We're trying to learn anything we can about who might be doing it. You don't happen to remember the people who dropped off the pizzas last time, do you? What they looked like?"

Sister Margaret frowned. Then she looked excited. "I didn't see the people myself, but one of our guests did. He told me there were two men wearing black. They came in a black hatchback. Does that help?"

Rita looked at Ben and smiled. "Sure does!" she said. Her phone jingled. "Wait a sec."

Rita answered the phone. "Yeah, Sarge. Yeah. Yeah. Sure." She hung up.

"That was Sarge," she said to Ben. "He wants us back at the station. You gotta sign some paperwork today, on account of it being your first day." She turned back to Sister Margaret. "Sorry, Mags. We don't have time for tea."

"Another time then," said Sister Margaret. "Come back anytime, you two. Hope you find the pizza."

"It looks like the pizza trail is cold." Ben snickered at his own joke.

Sister Margaret laughed out loud.

"That's pretty good," Rita said, as she sauntered back to the squad car. "You're going to fit in."

Ben swelled with pride. That was the one thing he wanted to do more than anything else in the world.

*

Back at the station, Ben met with Sarge. He was given paperwork to fill out. When that was done, Patty showed him where his locker was and where the lunchroom was. She introduced him to a few of the other guys. They seemed nice. So many names…he didn't know how he would keep them straight.

Then Patty took him back to Sarge.

"So," said Sarge. "How did your first day go? How did you get along with Officer Mom?"

"Great," Ben said, happily. "She's so nice."

The smile on Sarge's face twisted. "This must be some new meaning of the word 'nice' that you kids use. Like 'sick.'" He shook his head. "How is the pizza case going?"

Ben brought him up to date. He told Sarge that they planned to visit Meatsa Pizza first thing tomorrow.

"Well, you get on home now," said Sarge. "Looks like tomorrow is going to be a big day."

Ben left the station with a smile on his face.

Day 2

Chapter Nine

Ben was so anxious to get to work the next day that he arrived early. He wasn't the first, though. As soon as he entered the station, a voice rang out.

"There you are!" Rita yelled across the room. "Come on. Let's get rolling."

Ben followed her out to the parking lot.

"I don't talk much until I have my third coffee," said Rita. "We'll stop for one after we get to Vinnie's. I got a funny feeling about today."

About ten minutes later, Rita pulled the squad car up in front of Meatsa Pizza. They weren't alone. A small group of people stood in front of the main window, waving their arms excitedly.

"Crap. I was right." Rita got out of the car and yelled, "Hey, what's going on?"

A chubby man with gray hair bolted out of the crowd. His apron was stained with red sauce.

"Rita! Thank God you're here. *Mamma mia*, look what they did!" He pushed aside people to make a path for Rita.

Ben followed. Someone had thrown at least three large pails of tomato sauce at the front window.

"They must have done it just before I got here. I came in the back way. I only just got here, and this is what I found. It's still wet. You can see it from the inside. My beautiful window!"

It wasn't very beautiful right now. Ben thought it looked like one of those abstract paintings that people pay stupid amounts of money for. Either that or blood. He shivered.

Vinnie flailed his arms. "Look at this! And look what it did to the flowers below. What a mess! Why, Rita? Why? I didn't do nothing." The poor fellow was close to tears.

"It's that Tony O. Or his son Rocco." Some guy started yacking in Italian. A few others joined in. They made quite a racket. Ben couldn't understand a word.

"No, it isn't!" said a very pretty young lady in the doorway. She had long dark brown hair and huge eyes. "Rocco didn't do it! He wouldn't!"

The shouting in Italian got louder.

Rita spoke quietly to Ben. "Ho ho, So I see the rumors are true."

"What rumors?" said Ben.

"About Rocco and Julia." Rita whispered in his ear. "Rocco is Tony O's son. Julia is Vinnie's daughter."

"Rocco and Julia?" Ben asked. "You mean like Romeo and Juliet?"

Rita nodded.

Ben groaned. He remembered taking Romeo and Juliet in school. It was so sad. The warring families. Kids in love, caught in the cross-fire. It didn't turn out well. Was this some kind of pizza war between modern day feuding families?

This day was already turning into a soap opera. Or some kind of opera.

"Julia!" Vinnie's voice cut through the chatter. "Do you know something about this?"

Julia was indignant. "I know Rocco from school. You know he goes to church, Papa. Rocco would never do anything to hurt your business. He has too much respect for you."

"Oh," Vinnie sounded confused. "Well, then."

Respect was important in Italian families, Ben knew.

Vinnie thought for a moment. "I really can't believe Tony Orso is behind a thing like this. It doesn't make sense. Not now. After the food fight at the funeral, maybe. That was a lot of wasted food. You know what a cheapskate he is. But that was ages ago. Why now?"

Rita walked up to the window. "I agree. This doesn't seem like something Tony Orso would do. He hates to waste food." She reached out a finger and swiped up some sauce. Before anyone could say anything, she stuck it in her mouth.

Rita frowned. She swirled the sauce in her mouth. Finally, she said. "Not enough oregano. This isn't Tony's sauce. Try it."

Vinnie stepped forward, reached down toward the window sill, and scooped up some sauce with his fingers. They went into his mouth.

"You're right," said Vinnie, looking relieved. "He didn't do it."

"Maybe he used someone else's sauce?" Ben tried to be helpful.

Everyone shook their heads.

"Nah," said Vinnie, wiping fingers on his white apron. "He wouldn't do that. Blame someone else? The guy pulled a dirty trick and stole my girl. But he's like me! He has his pride."

A short guy nearby nodded. *They all seemed to work for Vinnie*, Ben thought.

Then everyone started to talk at once. They appeared to agree, but he couldn't be sure. No doubt about it. Ben was going to have to learn Italian.

"You're right, Rita. He's too cheap to waste sauce. You know the ring he gave Vera was only gold plated?" He grunted in disgust.

Ben groaned. *Here we were, back to 1985 again.*

Rita looked thoughtful. "So if Tony Orso didn't do this, who *did*?" Rita asked.

They looked at each other. "And who is stealing all those pizzas from Tony O's?" asked Ben. "Is it the same guy who did this? Someone who is trying to hurt them both?"

"Might be," said Rita. She punched him on the arm. "Yup, it looks that way. Maybe somebody is trying to drive them *both* out of business. Nice work, Ben. You got a brain. Let me think."

The crowd became quiet.

Rita frowned as she thought. Wrinkles formed on her forehead. Her mouth became a thin line. Then her eyes went wide. Ben waited. And waited.

Finally, she said, "Well, there's only one way to tell who is doing this."

"What's that?" said Vinnie.

Her smile was devious. "We're going to set a trap."

Chapter Ten

Rita had missed her third cup of coffee. "Let's stop at Timmy's for a cup of joe and a bite," she said.

"What's at Timmy's?" asked Ben.

"Just the best coffee and donuts this side of the planet!" She pulled up in front of a very busy fast-food place on Main. She managed to get the last free parking spot.

Ben followed her into the place. It was packed. They went to stand in line.

"My treat," said Rita. "You find a table."

Ben found a little two-seater by a window. He watched people come and go. Everyone looked happy. Rita came back with two coffees, double cream, no sugar.

"Save the sugar for these donuts," she said, plunking herself down. "They're the best."

She's right about that, Ben thought. The coffee was good too. No wonder everyone left happy!

They munched for a while, slurping coffee between bites. When his donut was all gone, Ben broke the silence.

"So does Vinnie know about Rocco and Julia?" Ben asked.

"Nah," said Rita. "Fathers are blind when it comes to love. I think the mothers know. I heard it from Julia's mother's hairdresser."

Ben nodded. He was beginning to think police should go undercover in hair salons.

Still, he sighed. It was romantic, in a way. The children of pizza rivals finding love with each other. So much in common. Think of all they could share! Children…recipes…little baby pizzas…

He was just about finished his coffee when Rita said, "Ready to go?"

He nodded. They gathered up the garbage, and prepared to leave.

"About that trap you mentioned," Ben said.

"Yes," Rita said. "So here's what I've been thinking…"

Before she could finish the sentence, her cell phone jingled.

It was Tony Orso. She put it on speaker so Ben could hear.

"Rita? That you? *Mamma mia*! Cockroaches!!"

"What?" Rita yelled into the phone. "What about cockroaches?"

"All over the floor! On the counters! Running everywhere!"

Ben heard someone scream in the background.

"Making a meal of the mozzarella! You gotta come! Some guy let go a bunch of cockroaches in the front of the restaurant while I was in the back! What am I gonna do? I'll be ruined!"

"Oh, my God. Calm down, Tony. Can you hold? I got another call coming in."

Ben waited as Rita switched to the new caller.

"Rita! Get back here! Rats!!" said Vinnie. His voice was frantic.

"What?" said Rita.

"Rats in the dining room! Some guy just came in and left a bag of rats! They're running all over the place!" Vinnie's voice ended in a sob.

"Did you see who it was?" said Rita.

"Nope. We were all in the back. I could hear the door open and then close. When I went to see who it was—" Vinnie said. Then, his voice was drowned out by people screeching.

"OK, Vinnie. We'll be there as soon as we can."

*

Rita decided they would drive to Vinnie's first because it was closer.

When they got to Meatsa Pizza, a bunch of people were standing outside. Vinnie, Julia, and a few people Ben hadn't seen before were talking.

A beat-up old car had pulled up just ahead of them. A good-looking young man climbed out of the driver's seat. He opened the back seat door and pulled out a cage.

Julia gasped. "Rocco! What are you doing here?"

Rocco looked triumphant. "I'm here to trap the rats so they'll eat the cockroaches."

"What? Whata you say?" Vinnie wasn't the only one confused. Even Rita looked baffled.

"That's really quite smart," said Ben. Finally, something he knew about. "Rats eat anything. They'll eat cockroaches. So Rocco can trap the rats here, and take them over to Tony O's to eat the cockroaches."

"Kill two birds with one stone, as they say," Rita said, nodding.

"That's such a good idea, Rocco!" Julia clapped her hands. "I'm so glad I called—oops." She slapped a hand to her mouth.

Ben smiled. Julia had obviously called Rocco to tell him about the rats. Rocco looked at Julia with such longing in his eyes. It was hard to imagine that her father Vinnie didn't notice. Maybe if this rat trap worked, Vinnie would be OK with the romance.

"Good thinking," said Rita. "Then we can go to the Humane Society to get some cats to take care of the rats. They can spare some. They have enough."

Everyone nodded.

"You guys set your rat traps. I'm going to set my own. For the biggest rats of all. Vinnie, don't you worry much. I got a plan," she said. "I can't tell you, because it's gotta be secret. You trust me?"

Vinnie agreed immediately. So did Julia. So did Rocco.

Rita looked at Ben and grinned. "Time to rock and roll, partner." She pulled him back over to the squad car.

Once inside, she took out her phone. She glanced at Ben. "I'm calling Tony O now."

When Tony answered, Rita started to talk. "Listen Up, Tony. You heard about the rats at Vinnie's? Yeah…yeah. I'm going to set a trap. Here is what I want you to do." She spent the next few minutes outlining the plan.

Chapter Eleven

They cleared the plan with Sarge back at the station.

Ben gabbed with Patty and the officers on desk duty for a while. They all seemed friendly. He ate lunch and then wrote up his first report.

It was mid-afternoon when Tony called to say the van was ready.

"Let's go," Rita said to Ben.

About fifteen minutes later, Rita pulled into the little alley around the back of Tony O's. A van was waiting, along with two people. Tony was one. He waved them over.

Rita parked the squad car off to the side, and they both got out.

"I loaded it with twenty empty pizza boxes," Tony told Rita. "Just like you said."

Rita surveyed the back of the van. "And you yelled out loud that you were doing this? Just in case they planted a bug in the dining room and were listening in."

He smiled proudly. "Yup! Complained real loud about last minute orders. Right, Donna?"

His waitress Donna nodded. "I pretended to have a tantrum about having to work on my lunch break." She wiped her hands on her apron. "We locked all the food up in the freezer so the cockroaches wouldn't get at it."

Ben thought, *I hope the pizza boxes in the back of the van aren't full of cock-*

roaches. On second thought, the thieves would get a nice shock if they were. Imagine a new pizza special: pepperoni with mushrooms and cockroaches.

"Close those doors, Ben, and let's roll," Rita said.

He closed the heavy back doors of the van and climbed into the passenger seat.

Rita started the ignition.

"So what's the plan now?" said Ben.

"We drive around town, taking the sideroads," said Rita. "That Tony O's logo on the side of the van is easy to spot. If the rotten punks were listening in, they'll know we've left by now. I don't think it will take long."

She gave him a side glance. "I should probably tell you this could get nasty."

Ben took a big breath. This was what he had signed up for. He wanted to make a difference. This would be his first chance. Still, he was nervous.

"Can we do it, just the two us?" Ben asked.

"Two of them. Two of us. They're only punks. Sure, we can." Rita spoke with confidence. She even started to hum a tune. Ben was pretty sure he'd heard it somewhere before. *Was it a theme from a cowboy movie?*

Rita turned onto a side street. And then onto another. They weren't in the van more than ten minutes when it happened.

A black hatchback came out of nowhere. It swerved in front of them, blocking the way. Rita had to slam on the brakes to keep from hitting it.

Two young guys dressed in black bolted out of the car. They ran to the back of the van.

"It's showtime!" said Rita, as she leapt out of the van. Ben followed her as fast as he could.

"Stop! It's the police!" Rita yelled. Ben raced to her side.

The two guys had opened the back. They looked up at her command.

"Hands off those pizza boxes!" said Rita.

The bigger one laughed. "This?" he said. "This is who they send to stop us?"

Uh oh, thought Ben.

Rita stood her ground. "I don't know you, and I know all the punks in this town. So who are you bums working for?"

"Wouldn't you like to know?" The biggest one sneered at her. He leaned back against the van and crossed his arms.

Rita kept her cool. In fact, she went cold as ice.

"Yes, I *would* like to know," Rita replied.

Boy, that voice is chilling, Ben thought. Every part of him tingled, waiting for what would happen next.

"Yeah, so what're you going to do about it, old lady?" sneered the young punk. He took a step forward.

Old lady? Everyone froze. Ben's hands became fists. He held his breath, ready to step in if Rita needed help.

Rita glared at the guy. "It's time somebody taught you some manners," she said.

What happened next became a legend in Steeltown.

Rita released the weapon from her belt. She twirled in the air with the wooden spoon held high. She smacked the punk across the mouth, clobbered his nose, thumped him around the ears, and pounded his head. She was a whirling like a ninja.

Whack! Bam! Pow! The young guy held his head in his hands and yelped like a toddler.

It was over in two minutes. A smash between the legs brought him down to his knees. A few more spoons across the rear took him to the pavement.

Some people had gathered to watch. Ben and everyone else just stood there, speechless.

Rita hadn't needed help.

"You can keep the pizzas," said the other guy. He tiptoed backwards and then ran off.

Rita turned back to the thief on the ground. "So I'll ask you again. Who are you working for?" She brandished the wooden spoon over him.

"Pee Pee," he managed to squeak out.

"Pee Pee?" Ben repeated.

"Pee Party," gasped the guy on the ground.

"Oh. Pizza Party," said Rita. "Well, I'll be damned. That new company from south of here. So they're trying to muscle in on Steeltown territory, are they? Drive the locals out of business? In *my* town?"

Everyone waited. What was Rita going to do next?

She frowned. Her free hand clenched. And then her face cleared.

"As it happens, I hate paperwork. So does my boss. I've a mind to let you go with a warning. Make an example out of you." She waved her arm. "So here's the plan. Go back to your scuzzy employers. You tell them Mom says to get stuffed, and I don't mean cheesy pie crusts. They mess with Tony O's or Meatsa Pizza again, and I'll fry their fritters. I got a special rec- ipe." She smiled, and it wasn't nice.

Ben gulped. He wasn't the only one.

"I mean it." She stood right over the guy on the ground. "I don't like punks messing with my town. I got a reputation to uphold, see? So get your sorry butt back to whatever rock you crawled out from. And don't let me see you around here again."

She gave him a good stare, ready for round two. It wasn't needed. He was still whimpering on the ground.

Rita turned back to Ben and said, "I think our work here is done." She holstered the wooden spoon and headed to the van.

Ben followed her. He rushed forward to close the back doors of the van before she could tell him to do it.

There were so many questions he wanted to ask. How had she developed this skill? Could she teach it to him?

When the doors were bolted, Rita pulled him aside. It was like she was reading his mind.

"Probably you're wondering about the technique I used," said Rita. "When you got five kids—"

"Five kids?" repeated Ben.

"All boys." Rita sighed. "The little hoodlums. Why couldn't I have a girl? Just one girl? Some sweet little girl I could teach all my craft to."

Ben giggled. He couldn't help it. Sweet little girl? Who needed guns or knives when you had a wooden spoon?

"Back there. That was…" He searched for the word. "Amazing."

Rita nodded. "You punch him in the nose. That's police brutality. You whack him with a wooden spoon? Nobody says nothing."

She smiled. It looked scary.

"We'll get these pizza boxes back to Tony. Then," Rita looked at her watch. "Holy crap. Nearly shift change. We better get back to the station or we'll miss patty-cake." She grabbed his arm and ordered him into the passenger seat.

"Patty-cake?" Ben asked, bewildered. *The little kid's game? A lot of strange things had happened today, but this might take the cake.*

Rita hopped into the driver's seat. "Yeah. It's Tuesday. Patty's husband owns a bakery. On Tuesday, she brings in the leftover cakes that didn't sell. We gotta get back before the next shift eats it all, the greedy oinks."

"Yeah. The oinks!" said Ben. "Save our cake!"

"Darn right, Ben," said Rita. The van shifted into gear with a clunk. "You're going to fit in just fine."

Ben smiled. It was great to feel like he belonged.

www.ingramcontent.com/pod-product-compliance
Lightning Source LLC
Chambersburg PA
CBHW022114050726
47591CB00002B/787